super
HYPER
creative
HYPER COOL !!!!
I want
to play
little
mole
terrific
ah BLAH blah
non-stop
get ready!

For my brother Tito and my daughter Martina, with love
Anna Llenas

A TEMPLAR BOOK

First published in Spain under the title *Topito Terremoto* by Penguin Random House.
First published in the UK in 2018 by Templar Publishing,
an imprint of Kings Road Publishing, part of the Bonnier Publishing Group,
The Plaza, 535 King's Road, London, SW10 0SZ
www.bonnierpublishing.com

Text and illustrations copyright © Anna Llenas 2017
www.annallenas.com

1 3 5 7 9 10 8 6 4 2

ISBN 978-1-78741-230-9 (hardback)
ISBN 978-1-78741-231-6 (paperback)

This book was typeset in Meta
The illustrations were created with acrylic and collage

English translation: © Marta Fenollar 2017
English translation edited by Katie Haworth and Phoebe Jascourt

Printed in Malaysia

LiTTLE MOLE is a whirlwind

ANNA LLENAS

templar
books

Deep underground,
everything is quiet . . .

. . . but then Little Mole wakes up!

Suddenly, it's not so peaceful anymore.
That's because Little Mole is a whirlwind.

He bounds! He bounces! He bellows!

Later, when Little Mole walks to school,
he is distracted by everything.

He's even more distracted in class.

"Today we will be starting your end-of-year projects," says the teacher.

Oh no! Little Mole isn't listening!

He can't stop moving!

He fiddles! He fidgets! He forgets!

Little Mole is a whirlwind.

His classmates avoid him, and he doesn't understand why . . .

They call him all sorts of names.

Sometimes he feels like he's wearing so many labels he doesn't know who he is.

His teacher is worried – no matter what she does, she can't help Little Mole focus.
She writes his parents a letter:

"Little Mole is having problems concentrating.
We need to help!"

His parents are exhausted.

"Punishing Little Mole and sending him to his room hasn't worked,"
says his mum. "There must be another solution!"

Just then, the newspaper is delivered. Inside there is a very interesting advert:

They head out to the forest straight away and find Serena.

"Our Little Mole is a whirlwind and he just can't concentrate," says Little Mole's dad. "Is there something wrong with him?"

"I think I can help!" smiles Serena. "Why don't you bring him to see me tomorrow after school?"

The next day, when Little Mole visits Serena, she asks him about his day.

He looks sad.

"What's the matter, Little Mole?"

He takes a deep breath. "I don't know what to do for my end-of-year project. I just mess everything up. I can never finish anything. And . . . and nobody ever wants to play with me."

Serena knows just what to do.
She takes Little Mole to a lovely room filled with
crayons and paints and paper.

"Every week let's try making
something different!" she suggests.
Little Mole likes this idea.

At first, he touches everything.

He spills! He splashes! He speeds!

He starts lots of projects, but doesn't finish anything – it's chaos!

But rather than stopping him, Serena asks if he'd like to help with her drawing.

Some days they play . . .

Some days they cook . . .

One evening they even look at the stars.

But most of the time they talk.
Little Mole tells Serena about his worries,
his hopes, his dreams and his fears . . .

MR. PÉREZ

Each time Little Mole comes to visit, he sits still for a bit longer.

And, after a few months, he realises that he has finished all sorts of things he never thought he could.

One day, Serena says, "don't you see Little Mole? You are just like this train . . . you need a track to follow so you don't go flying off!"

"And your track is what you most like to do
 – it's your passion."

"My passion?" asks Little Mole.

"Yes!" Serena replies. "And guess what?
There is nothing wrong with you at all.
You are wonderful just the way you are."

That evening, Little Mole works on his end-of-year project.

His parents can't believe their eyes.

At last, it's the final day of school – time for Little Mole's class to present their projects.

"Did you bring anything, Little Mole?" they ask him.

Little Mole leads everyone outside.

"Yes I did! Here it is and you can all have a piece!"

His classmates are very impressed. Little Mole has never felt happier – the world suddenly seems a much sweeter place.

super
HYPER
HYPER
COOL !!!
creative
I want
to play
little
mole
terrific
ah BLAH blah
non-stop
get ready!

Also by Anna Llenas:

I Love You (Nearly Always) picture book
ISBN: 978-1-78370-797-3

I Love You (Nearly Always) pop-up
ISBN: 978-1-78370-761-4

The Colour Monster picture book
ISBN: 978-1-78370-423-1

The Colour Monster: a pop-up book
ISBN: 978-1-78370-356-2

www.bonnierpublishing.com